Sea Breeze Junior School: FIGHT FOR IT!
An Osborne Publication

Published in Great Britain.

This edition was published 2021.

Set in 14/16pt Geneva.

Printed and distributed by Amazon.

For Florence and Arthur

SEA
BREEZE
JUNIOR SCHOOL

Luke Osborne

FIGHT FOR IT!

A girl's football adventure

SEA
BREEZE
JUNIOR SCHOOL

Chapter 1

First Day of School

September 4th had rolled around rather quickly. The day was here and Florence was set to go back to school once again. The summer holidays were officially over. But this time around the return to school feeling was far more exciting than it had ever been before.

Florence certainly wasn't sad to be back - she was over the moon!

She was standing at the entrance gates with her mum when her friends, Aanya and Hannah, ran up to her. It seemed she wasn't the only one to be excited. They entered the playground side by side and looked around in awe. Everything was new.

Day one at the Seabreeze Junior School was finally here.

The school building looked so big and exciting compared to their previous school.

Florence looked back and waved goodbye to her mum. The playground had a bike shed that ran along one side - it seemed all the big year sixes were 'hanging out' along there.

At the far side was a climbing wall, next to a fenced-off area filled with benches. In the middle of the playground were three huge basketball courts with shiny pads around the bottom of the posts. But more importantly, centre stage, there was the football pitch.

New goals.
New nets.
New freshly painted white lines.

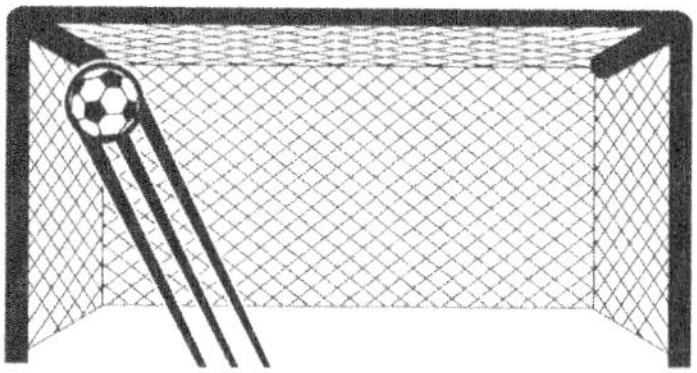

Already filled with boys, it wasn't the most inviting match to go and join in with.

"Maybe at break time there will be more space and we can play?" Florence asked.

Aanya and Hannah nodded.

Aanya was short and slight and had dark hair hanging on her shoulders. Hannah had freckles across her face and was slightly taller. Her blonde hair was quite a bit longer than both Florence and Aanya's.

"Yeah," Aanya said, "It is going to be AWESOME!"

"I don't think I'm going to be able to concentrate in class thinking about it," Hannah added.

The girls were never allowed to play football at their first school, not just the girls but the boys either. It was never played in PE and never set up for playtime either. The only time they got to play was on the weekend with their beloved Southern United. They knew they could play football at their new school, every break time, in lots of PE lessons and even at after school clubs!

Seabreeze Junior School was in the middle of a built-up town right on the seafront. You couldn't see the sea from the school but when the breeze was in the right direction you could smell it. Florence had spent much of her summer playing in the rock pools and jumping in the waves with her mum, dad and brother Arthur.

Although Florence lived in an area with many fields and parks nearby, she hadn't had a chance to meet up with her friends to play a real football match. Everyone is always busy with their families in the summer holidays and her football team didn't train during August.

It had been a long wait for today.

She had been dreaming of the start of the school term for months. It was the one place that she had known she would get to play football.

Every. Single. Day.

Her dad worked at the school and often when he had to pop in to prepare lessons during the holidays she had tagged along.

But being there with just her brother, Arthur, wasn't quite as exciting as a football pitch filled with children.

Over the blaring noise of excited children in the playground came a voice, "Hey guys! Are you excited for our first day?"

A girl with long dark hair stood next to the group. She was Florence's best friend Millie.

"I'm so excited. Do you know where we line up?" Florence said.

Just as Florence finished her question the playground bell rang out. The Headteacher was stood with his sunshades on looking tall. Florence had never known a male Headteacher before, in fact, she had never had any male teachers before!

As the bell rang, most of the older children started to gather in some sort of organised line. The new year threes, including the four friends, looked a little lost.

Their teacher appeared out of the door and waved a big sign with their class name on it. The word Peaches was written across the top of the sign and their teacher, Miss Hedges, was stood holding it. This was it. New school. New classroom. New teacher.

SEA BREEZE
JUNIOR SCHOOL

Chapter 2

First Break Time

"GOOOOALLLLLL!" shouted out one of the year 3 boys as his toe-poke slotted into the bottom corner. He ran over to his teammates to celebrate. It wasn't the World Cup Final but the joy on his face certainly came close.

It was break time and the playground was HEAVING with children. There were so many more children than at their old school. The football pitch was even busier. It was so busy in fact, that the ball often got lost in the sea of feet and legs. Florence wasn't even sure where the ball was most of the time.

The four friends were watching on from the sidelines. No girls were playing at the moment, just 45 screaming boys on a pitch not much bigger than a five a side pitch. Florence had often played football with the boys before but this was terrifying. It wasn't the kind of football the girls had come to love. It was brutal.

Break time was over in a flash and before they knew it they were back in the classroom. Miss Hedges came over to a sad-looking Millie.

“Everything ok at break time, Millie?”

“Yeah, everything was ok. We just didn’t have anything to do.” Millie replied.

“Surely there are loads of things to do! Climbing walls, basketball, chatting zones, running games and football. That’s quite a lot. Don’t you like any of that? I thought you liked football, girls?”

Millie shrugged and Aanya joined in the conversation.

“We do like those things, Miss Hedges. We LOVE football, but we didn’t want to play football with the boys. It was too busy and I don’t think they know what passing means.”

"Oh, I see. Well, the good news is that on Friday lunch play it is girl's football. Where only the girls are allowed to play." Miss Hedges smiled.

"Oh ok, we didn't know that. Thank you." Aanya said.

As lunchtime came around, the girls were sat in the quiet area. It was only Monday and they were quite saddened that their excitement of playing football every day at school wasn't going to be a reality. They knew they could join in with the boys if they wanted to but they didn't want to.

They barely got passed to; the boys would always make mean comments. When they did finally pass the ball it was as if they were doing the girls a favour by passing to them. It was as if it was the boy's pitch and the girls were just a nuisance. They wished they could have more break times to play football with just girls. Football at playtimes was meant to be fun, they were more than happy to play football with the boys in PE, just not at playtime.

"Maybe we could ask the Headteacher if we can have a second football pitch on the playground?" Hannah suggested.

Aanya finished off the last of her apple before replying, "Yeah, or maybe just have more break times where the girls get to play football alone!"

Florence was deep in thought.

“Well, what if we spoke to the Headteacher now? Mr Kilman is over there, look.” Florence pointed across the playground.

Mr Kilman was a tall man with large shoulders. He seemed to always be smiling and the girls had remembered him well from their tour of the school all those months ago.
“Afternoon girls! Are you having a great first day?” Mr Kilman beamed down at them.

“Oh yes Mr Kilman, a good day, thank you,” Hannah said.

"But we were wondering if maybe we could have a second pitch to play football on," asked Hannah.

"We don't want to play with the boys." Explained Millie.

"It isn't as fun for us," chipped in Florence.

"Oh right, well you can play on Friday. Every Friday lunch play the football pitch is just for girls." Mr Kilman stated.

"Yeah, that's what Miss Hedges said. We just thought we could play every day as the boys do," Hannah said.

"Can we have another ball and play football in the space on the playground over there instead?" Aanya pointed to space at the edge of the playground nearest the school. "I'm afraid not, we only allow one football on the playground at once. Too many balls flying around otherwise and it gets a bit dangerous. You should've seen what happened to Mrs Lourdes that time when we had multiple balls out here!" Mr Kilman had started to ramble on a bit. "Sorry girls, you'll just have to wait till Friday." Mr Kilman had been distracted by someone falling over and cutting their knee and walked away.

Aanya stood arms crossed. Hannah knew this stance.

Florence was rather angry, they all were.

"How is that fair? The boys hog the football pitch all week long and we only get to play once on a Friday? I know we COULD join in with the boys but there's no point. We might be on the football pitch but we won't get to actually PLAY football." Florence was ranting a little but felt better for getting it off her chest.

The girls joined with their class line and headed to the lunch hall. They sat there eating, none of them said a word for fifteen minutes.

SEA
BREEZE
JUNIOR SCHOOL

Chapter 3

The bouncing tooth

Back in the classroom after lunch, Miss Hedges said she had an exciting announcement to make.

"This afternoon we are going to nominate, and vote for, our Junior Governors. Junior Governors are two children chosen from each class. They get to represent the class in meetings with Mr Kilman to discuss things that happen at the school. Sometimes

Junior Governors can bring about real change to how we do things here. We will be voting for one girl and one boy. I will give you ten minutes to think of a few words that you want to say to the class if you want to run for the position. We will vote after everyone has spoken and I will announce the results before you go home today."

Florence looked like she had a plan.

She spoke quietly and looked at her friends, "How about I put myself forward for Junior Governor and we all vote for me? If I get voted in maybe I can convince Mr Kilman to change the way football is shared at playtimes!"

The girls thought it was a brilliant idea and they worked quickly to put together 3 key ideas that they felt would get enough votes to get Florence elected.

3 girls and 3 boys had put their names forward for the election. Each of them had a chance to talk for one minute and explain why they would be good in the role of Junior Governor.

Tamara went first. A taller girl with glasses and brown eyes. She towered over Ellie next to her, who was also keen to become Junior Governor.

"I suggest we run double English lessons every Friday so we can write even more in lessons..."

One of the boys groaned and was quickly spoken to, by Miss Hedges, for being rude.

"And I would like to see more seating on the playground for us children who just like to sit and read." Tamara finished off by saying she would also try to ban all football on the playground as there are too many injuries caused by the game.

There was a shocked look among a number of the children but some children seemed genuinely pleased by the suggestion.

Florence stood nervously at the front waiting her turn. She was also shocked about Tamara's idea to ban football at playtimes. Surely it wouldn't happen but what if it did? What if Tamara won and she managed to ban it!?

Florence knew some people didn't love football but never understood how they couldn't, she loved playing it! It wasn't just the excitement of scoring a goal, but the team working together, playing with her friends, learning new skills and tricks, coming up against new players, being strong and having endless fun - what wasn't there to love?

Miss Hedges asked Florence to speak next. Hannah, Aanya and Millie leant forward in their seats.

Florence held her notes in front of her and started to read from them, “I think I will be a good Junior Governor because I am not afraid to share my opinion and I will listen to all of your big ideas and tell Mr Kilman all about them. I believe in keeping things fair and will try my best to make sure boys and girls have the same chances as each other.”

The group of three jumped up and started clapping. In the short time they had together to work out their three points for the speech, they decided not to mention football.

The boys went next and then Miss Hedges told the children the rules on how to vote.

“I am going to get you to write a boy’s name and a girl’s name on the post-it note I give you. Try to keep it secret and remember to write the name of the boy and girl who you think will be the best for our class."

Florence was once again rather nervous. Maybe it was silly, but getting to play football at school truly was the most important thing in her life. At this moment in time nothing else mattered.

Miss Hedges asked the class to read their books whilst she added up all of the votes.

"Ok year 3, the votes are in! For the boys, you have elected...Bradley!"

The class clapped for their first Junior Governor. Bradley stayed seated and wiped his fringe across his forehead. He was a keen footballer, Florence knew that already. Quite tall, quick and excellent at Maths.

Aanya, who was sat in front of Bradley, turned round to face him, “Well done, Bradley.”

“Thanks,” came the confident reply.

“Now for the girls,” Miss Hedges spoke softly. “You have voted for...”

Hannah was sat forward on the edge of her seat, so much so she ended up planted straight onto the floor.

BANG!

Somehow in the movement, she managed to hit her chin hard onto the tabletop. Aanya was the one who spotted the tooth bounce across the carpet in front of her and scooped it up into a tissue.

By the time Hannah had been helped up and taken to the first aid room to be checked over, the end of the day had come and the announcement seemed to have been forgotten.

Millie put her hand up.

“Yes, Millie?” Miss Hedges asked.

“Are we going to find out who the other Junior Governor is going to be?” Millie asked.

“Ah yes, sorry. I almost forgot. We’ve got just about enough time to announce the winner. Our other Junior Governor for this year is going to be, Florence!"

Florence felt herself go red and was first to leave the room when Miss Hedges dismissed the class. Outside of the school gate Hannah was coming out of the front office with her mum and called out to the other 3 girls.

"How did it go? Did we win?" she quizzed the leaving group.

"Yeah, Florence is our Junior Governor! We will be able to get football every day now for sure," Aanya answered.

"Oh, that's brilliant! Why do you look so sad then Florence?" asked Hannah.

Florence shuffled a little, “Well, what if I can’t change anything? What if, even as Junior Governor, I can’t get what we want?”

The girls made Florence feel a little more confident with their group’s secret handshake. It had been mastered in a holiday camp in the summer holidays. The girls then said their goodbyes and headed over to their waiting parents.

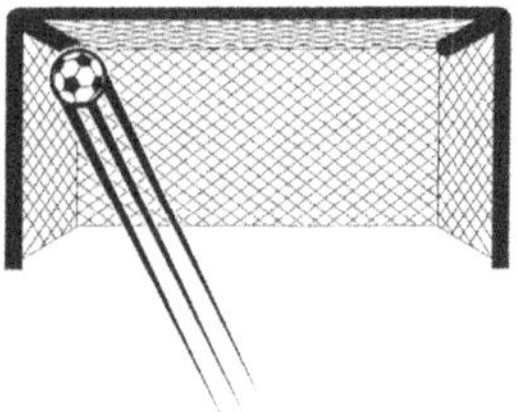

SEA
BREEZE
JUNIOR SCHOOL

Chapter 4

Friday Break Time

"Good morning everyone!" Mr Kilman addressed the whole school who were sat crossed legged in front of him ready for their first assembly.

Mr Kilman looked out across the whole hall, "Well we have almost completed our first week in school together and I must say, what a week so far! I have been so impressed with everyone. From the oldies up in year 6, showing the rest of you how it is done, down to the year 3's who have made it seem like they have been here for years!"

The Headteacher went on to discuss the exciting things that were coming up across the school year. A couple of things sparked special interest from the footballing foursome sat in the third row.

Mr Kilman continued, "Next week we will be starting football after school clubs, where everyone is welcome to attend. We will be picking the school football team for the first competitions of the year from those who come as well."

Mr Kilman paced along the front row before carrying on, "Year 3 boys and girls will be this Monday. Make sure your parents check their apps to sign up digitally - you no longer need to remember paper permission slips!"

At the end of the assembly, Mr Kilman said that if any of the children had any questions about the football clubs to ask their teachers back in their classroom. He also announced the Junior Governors for every class and got them to stand up.

Florence was super embarrassed but stood up as the rest of the school clapped the 40 newly elected Junior

Governors.

On the walk back to class all the talk was about the football club.

“Are you going to go?” Hannah whispered to the others.

“Of course I’m going to go!” Aanya was practically bursting with excitement.

“Shhhhhhh,” came the teacher’s voice from the front.

“Has your mum got the app to sign up?” Florence asked.

“Yeah, but they only got it last night, Dad’s useless at computers. Luckily Mum knows what she is doing!” laughed Millie.

Maths followed the assembly and seemed particularly hard that day. It was to do with measuring things in the classroom and then changing the measurement from centimetres into metres. But the girls were not paying enough attention.

Hannah kept staring through the window.

Their classroom looked out straight onto the football pitch, it had been a bit of a tease all week long - watching the boys playing every day. The weather had been glorious so far as well. She wanted break time to come soon.

“Ok everyone, tidy up your places and then you can head out to break.” Miss Hedges announced the words that were music to the ears of the girls desperate to play.

“YES!” called a voice from the back. The foursome turned to see Lily fist pump the air. They didn’t know Lily loved football that much.

Mr Kilman was standing on the football pitch as the girls started to arrive. He lined up the 14 girls and put them into two teams of 7. The girls were so excited they stood there in complete silence until the game started.

Florence, Millie and Hannah had been put on the same side but Aanya was on the other team with Lily, who was keen to be the goalkeeper. The girls were a bit disappointed but Aanya didn’t mind.

Mr Kilman was enjoying watching the girls play. The atmosphere on the pitch was wonderful as they knocked the ball around.

"So much calmer than the boy's football," he thought to himself.

1-0!

Hannah had opened the scoring, finishing after a mazy run, taking on 3 defenders and slotting it past Lily in goal. From the kick-off, Aanya was set up for a long-range shot which cracked off the crossbar.

"WOAH! What a shot Aanya, well done!" Mr Kilman bellowed. He was starting to get into this now, he was amazed at the quality of the game.

Millie had won a corner and had signalled to Florence for 'the routine'. It had been a while since they had linked up from a corner. Back in the summer, they had played in an U7s tournament and Millie had laid the ball out to Florence to shoot first time with the side of her foot. As the ball was about to come in, Florence remembered her coach's words, "controlled and accurate."

Millie stroked the ball across from the right side of the pitch, to the edge of the box, and Florence side-footed it straight into the bottom left of the goal. 2-0 now.

Another whoop from Mr Kilman was heard in the background as the goalkeeper, Lily, rolled the ball back to the centre circle for kick-off. A minute later, a rocket of a shot from Aanya flew in after a lay off from her teammate and straight in under the crossbar.

2-1.

Aanya wasn't a fan of dribbling with the ball or even passing but she could kick a ball harder than any of the other girls and she LOVED defending. That was her thing.

Mr Kilman rang the bell to signal the end of playtime and they headed to their lines.

"It felt so good to be playing again, didn't it," Aanya said to Hannah as they headed to the line. Mr Kilman was standing at the front with Miss Hedges and looked very excited.

"What are they talking about?" Millie said, nudging Florence.

"No idea," Florence replied turning her attention back to the front of the line.

After school that day Florence had to wait in her Dad's classroom until he was finished and ready to go home.

"Had a good day, Florence?" Florence's dad asked.

"Yeah we got to play football and I scored a goal and Aanya hit the crossbar and we won 3-1 and it was so much fun..." Florence burst out with noise and excitement, so quickly, that her Dad struggled to keep up.

"Woah! Slow down! You sound like you had a great playtime then." He thought for a second, before adding, "Of course, it is Friday, girl's football day!"

Her Dad was just finishing off putting some of the children's work on display when Miss Hedges came to the classroom door.

"Oh hi Luke, Hi Florence, had a good day?" Miss Hedges asked Florence's dad.

"Yeah great day thanks, Holly. You had a good one?" her Dad replied.

Florence smiled at her and then made herself look busy playing a snakes game on the class iPad.

"Yeah good, I have a lovely new class and I'm excited about getting started with football club on Monday." Miss Hedges then turned her attention to Florence, "Are you coming Florence?"

"Yeah," Florence answered quietly, hiding her obvious excitement.

Miss Hedges smiled at her, "I thought you'd say that, Mr. Kilman told me how well all of you girls played at break time today. He thinks we might have a chance at winning the big tournament in November!"

Florence was VERY interested in what Miss Hedges was saying but hid it well. She was always slightly shy in front of teachers at school when the other children had gone home and just smiled back.

Miss Hedges turned back to Florence's Dad, "Have you signed her up to the club yet Luke?"

“No, not yet. Can I just let you know she can come?” he replied.

“Oh no, you better do it on the app - you know how funny the office staff can be about doing it using the magical app!” Miss Hedges said with a smile.

“Oh, they are funny about their app!” He laughed, closing down his computer. “So you fancy your chances at beating St John’s this year then?”

“Let's see how we get on on Monday, it would be amazing. The first-ever Year Three girl’s football champions for our school. Could you imagine?” Miss Hedges thoughts trailed off as she walked away. “Have a nice weekend!”

After Florence was certain Miss Hedges was far enough away, she put down the iPad and turned to her dad.

"Does Miss Hedges run the girl's football team then?"

"Yeah, didn't she say?" her dad said whilst rinsing out his coffee cup.

"No, but if she runs the girl's football team why doesn't she want the girls to play more football at break time? Surely it would make us better players." Florence said.

"Alright, calm down Junior Governor! It isn't up to Miss Hedges to change, it is a decision for Mr Kilman."

As soon as Florence got home that night she called Hannah on her dad's phone.

"Guess who the girl's football coach is for the year threes?" Florence asked.

Before Hannah could even reply Florence had answered her own question, "MISS HEDGES!"

"Wait, really? I didn't know she knew anything about football," Hannah was as surprised and excited as Florence by the news.

"Me neither, Dad said about it and she's done it for years but she has never won a competition with the year three team. He said they've always come close but never quite made it." Florence was trying to hold the conversation whilst completing her spellings homework.

"Well, my mum ALWAYS says it isn't about winning it is about having fun with your friends and trying your best," Hannah said. "But I like the winning part too!"

"Me too," came the short reply. "Right, that's me finished now, I'll see you later."

"Bye, Florence. See you at the park Sunday," came the reply.

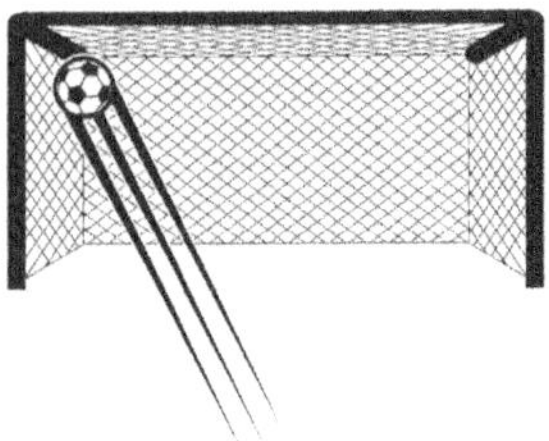

SEA BREEZE
JUNIOR SCHOOL

Chapter 5

First Football Club Day!

Monday morning was always a frantic one. Florence was a little flustered due to the excitement that was to come after school. She had told her Dad that she wanted to leave for school when he left, at 6:45 AM.

It was 6:43 AM.

Florence was still in her PJs.

She had prepared her school bag the night before and the reason she hadn't changed yet was that she had kept checking she had everything. She had checked it 15 times that morning already.

"Sorry Florence, you'll have to go with Mummy this morning. I'm ready to go now," her Dad insisted.

"I'm coming, I'm coming," Florence called from her bedroom.

Out of nowhere, she surfaced fully dressed, a football kit bag on her left shoulder and a book bag on her right shoulder.

Dad was shocked, "Blimey, that was quick."

“Don’t forget your lunch box and to say goodbye to your brother, Florence!” her mum called from the kitchen.

“Bye Arthur!” Florence called out.

Arthur came running into the hallway, “byyyyyyeeeeeeeeeeeeeee Floooooooooreeeeenncce!”

He ran into her, squeezing her so tight that he almost sent her (and her bags) flying into the air. Arthur loved a cuddle with his sister, Florence didn’t always love a cuddle with her brother though!

The school day seemed to last FOREVER.

9-10AM - History (Romans)
10-10:20AM - Break time (No Football)
10:20-11:20AM - Maths (Division)
11:20-12:20PM - English (Grammar)
12:20-12:45PM - Reading time
12:45-1:00PM - Lunch play
1:00-1:20PM - Lunch time
1:20-2:20PM - Art (Watercolours)
2:20-2:45PM - Spellings

The four girls had spent most of the day staring at the clock waiting for 2:45 PM to come round. Florence had enjoyed the Art lesson but even though that was her favourite lesson of the day, it had still dragged.

“Ok, if you are staying at school today for the football club, boys head to the changing rooms, girls you are to get changed in here today. As we have so many children joining us after school we needed to alter where you get changed."

Miss Hedges was suddenly wearing her PE kit.

"She had that kit on all day?" Aanya asked, whilst pulling her socks up.

"Yeah, I think so? Or maybe she got changed at lunchtime and we didn't notice?" replied Millie.

"It's a mystery!" Laughed Lily and both girls laughed back at her.

"Yeah! Maybe she's Superwoman? Quick jump into the art room cupboard, super spin and then back out again!" Florence said whilst still laughing.

The four friends had quickly become a group of five now with Lily. They all seemed to get on so well. Lily had red hair and was about the same height as Millie. She was always looking for a way to make a joke.

SEA
BREEZE
JUNIOR SCHOOL

Chapter 6

After school: The First Club

The girl's looked brilliant in their different football team tops, all from different teams across the country. Some had chosen to wear their PE kit instead, which Miss Hedges had said was fine to do. Florence was kitted out in her Brighton shirt with her name across the back, Millie and Hannah were Chelsea fans and Aanya supported West Ham.

Lily was wearing a brightly coloured Watford goalkeeper top, “I don’t even like Watford! But my Nan is a big fan and bought it for me, couldn’t say no, could I?!”
The field was looking fantastic, the grass had been freshly mown and the lines repainted. The feel of the soft grass underneath Florence’s cleaned football boots was incredible, she thought. They weren’t clean because Florence had been scrubbing them, it was because the 4g pitch that the girls had played on at the weekend always left their boots spotlessly polished.

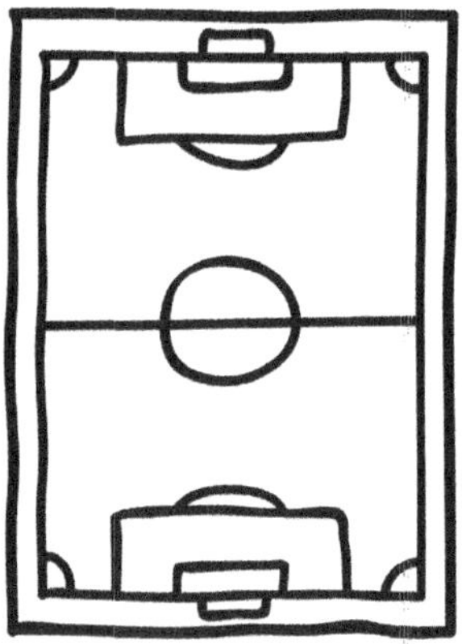

The boys were called over by Mr Parkinson,

who was on the far side of the pitch. Miss Hedges blew her whistle and the girls gathered around her on the smaller pitch. There were 18 girls at the club, Florence noted. Most of the girls there had played football at playtime on the previous Friday but there were others, she didn't recognise.

Lily was there, kitted out with her gloves and yellow Watford top. Of course Hannah, Aanya and Millie were there but Florence was surprised to see Tamara and Ellie, from her class, ready to go as well.

Miss Hedges flicked up a ball, over her head, and into her hands.
"WOAH, Miss Hedges, you're amazing!" called out Millie.

“Not bad for a teacher, eh girls?” she smiled. “Right girls, everyone get a football and get dribbling in this space over here. Just get a feel for the ball under your feet.”

The girls worked through several dribbling practices and then moved onto passing and shooting. For the final part of the club, the girls played some 5 a side matches.

“I want everyone to take turns being in goal. As there are only 5 players on each team you should stay active and be ready to help your team.”

After the club, Florence’s dad drove her home.

“How was it then?” he quizzed.

"Yeah really good fun, I wonder if I will get in the team for the first match," Florence said.

"Well if you don't, there's always next time! You just have to trust that Miss Hedges knows what she's doing," her dad replied.

Florence looked into their lounge window when they got home and knocked hard, making her brother Arthur jump out of his skin. He came running to the door to let both Florence and her Dad in.

The next morning there was a notice up in the classroom:

Year 3 School Teams

The following children have been chosen to play against St. John's in a friendly next week.

Your parents will be sent a notification via the app with further details

Boys Team:	Girls Team
Bradley	Sally
Tom	Florence
Albert	Hannah
Jack	Millie
Ronnie	Tamara
Harry	Martha
Elliot	Willow

SEA
BREEZE
JUNIOR SCHOOL

The girls were buzzing with excitement to see their names up on the notice board. Except for Aanya, the others hadn't noticed straight away - she wasn't on the team.

"Oh, Aanya, your name isn't on the list," Millie noted.

"Yeah, well, I don't care," a sad Aanya replied.

Miss Hedges approached the girls and had already anticipated the disappointment. "Morning girls, don't worry Aanya there will be lots of matches this year and everyone will get a chance to play in the school team. I could only take 7 girls sadly. You'll be invited next time."

Aanya knew that Miss Hedges hadn't left her out to upset her and was trying to make her feel better. However she didn't feel any happier for it, but smiled at her teacher anyway. She then slumped into a seat at her table ready for Maths.

SEA
BREEZE
JUNIOR SCHOOL

Chapter 7

The Friendly

Aanya had got over the initial disappointment and had still enjoyed going to the club, despite not being selected for the first school team of the year. The girl's had enjoyed their Friday break time as well.

Florence was pleased that Aanya wasn't upset anymore but was still sad that the five friends weren't playing together against St. Johns.

That afternoon, the 7 girls selected for the match met up in their classroom, 3 Peach, to start getting dressed. Miss Hedges and Mr Kilman were there looking rather pleased with themselves.

"To celebrate the first friendly match of the season girls, we thought we would give to you a brand new kit!" announced Mr Kilman.

They started handing out the shirts, double-checking sizes to make sure they fitted perfectly. The girls were so excited as they ripped open the airtight bags and pulled the tags off their new matching team wear.

On the school pitch the girls were warming up, kicking the ball to each other. It was Ellie who noticed St. Johns arrive first, the brilliant red of their kit emerged from across the field.

Florence noted that the 7 girls were marching in an almost perfect line, with their parents coming behind. At the front of the line was their teacher. He had long hair, was wearing an old fashioned pair of black boots and black socks which were over the top of his loose jogging bottoms. He was also wearing a long-sleeved collared shirt and a big red coat which stretched down past his knees.

“Is that their teacher?” Hannah asked.

Millie was staring, wide-mouthed, "Yeah, that must be him. Miss Hedges said he had a unique style." Both the girls giggled.

"I'm just going to say hello to Mr Silverthorn and sort out the start time. You girls keep passing the ball and stay warm."

Miss Hedges, kitted out in her co-ordinated Seabreeze Junior School kit, walked over to Mr Silverthorn and shook his hand.

"Afternoon Simon, everything ok?" she asked.

"Oh yes, we are all ready to go. I'll get the girls warmed up and then we can kick off straight away," he replied.
"Fifteen minutes each way seem ok?" Miss Hedges suggested. "It is just a friendly and

my girls haven't been playing together for very long."

Mr Silverthorn started shaking his head, "Oh no no, we need to play according to the FA guidelines. Twenty minutes each way. It may not mean anything to you but every game is a serious affair for St. Johns."

Miss Hedges rolled her eyes at him, but he didn't notice, "I am sure that's just guidance from the FA. But ok, that's fine. I'll just rotate the girls frequently."

Millie took the kick-off and passed it across to the right side of the pitch where Florence was waiting, she immediately pushed the ball straight down the wing beating the first defender. She looked up to see Millie had run with her and was about to enter the top of the goalkeeper's area, she laid it straight into Millie's path who side-footed the ball with ease past the goalkeeper. The whole of St. Johns looked bewildered.

Miss Hedges made a small 'yelp' as the ball crossed the line and Mr Silverthorn turned to her, "looks like you have got a good team this year then, beginners luck maybe?" Miss Hedges once again rolled her eyes, out of his view of course.

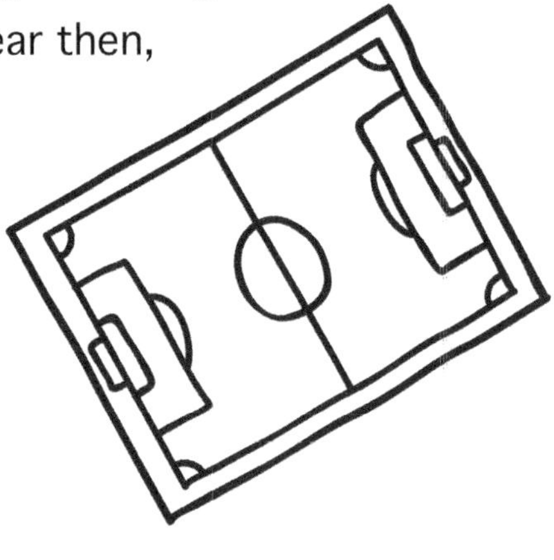

A quick high five between the

girls and they got back into position ready for kick-off. Hannah was fast off the blocks. As soon as St. Johns played their first pass, she regained possession in seconds. She played the ball between the two defenders for Millie to run on to but the defender managed a block which led to the first corner of the game.

The girls knew what to do, they had practised corners more than anything. Hannah looked up to see Florence hovering about the halfway line, as she went to play it Florence had made her run forward. The defenders hadn't noticed her.

Mr Silverthorn called out, "Get her! She's not marked!" It was too late though. Florence controlled the ball with her first touch and struck the ball with her second, sending the ball into the now bulging net.

Seabreeze Junior School 2 - 0 St. Johns
Millie ‘1
Florence ‘5

“Right,” called Mr Silverthorn, “we’ve had enough of this. Amy get ready.”

Miss Hedges turned to see an extremely tall girl taking her jumper off. She was almost as tall as her.

“I know she is tall, but she is a year three.” Mr Silverthorn said reading Miss Hedges’ mind.

“Oh I don’t doubt it,” Miss Hedges replied smiling at Amy, “Good luck in the game Amy,” Miss Hedges added.

There was still 15 minutes left of the first half, it had been a great start for Seabreeze but there was a long way to go in the match.

Kick-off again, this time the ball was passed across to Amy who held off Hannah’s attempt to win the ball with her big frame and smashed the ball from just inside the halfway line. The whole pitch of girls, and the supporters, stood and stared as the ball sailed through the air and hit the top corner of the goal.

Seabreeze Junior School 2 - 1 St. Johns
Millie '1 Amy '6
Florence '5

Mr Silverthorn jumped in the air, "YES! There we go."

Then another. 2-2.

Then another. 2-3.

Despite Seabreeze managing one attack before half time, the first half finished 2-3 to St. Johns.

Miss Hedges tried her best to rally the troops. "Come on girls, don't be so down. Yeah, she's a good player but we can play around her. St. Johns can still be beaten!"

"I wonder who she plays for outside of school, I've never seen her before," Florence said.

"I wouldn't worry about that girls, or the score line. Your first five minutes was brilliant, and no matter the scoreline at the end of the day this is just a fun match; a chance to practice playing as a school team against other schools." Miss Hedges remained upbeat.

Hannah stepped forward, "Yeah, come on girls, we've been losing by more than this before and still won. We just need to play like we always do."

Miss Hedges had made two changes ready for the second half, with Willow and Martha coming on in place of Tamara and Millie.

St. Johns kicked off. Amy scored in seconds. Hitting the ball so hard this time it flew in off the goalkeeper's head. This was Sally's first-ever football match against another team. She had often played football at home with her Dad and LOVED playing in goal. The whole family were so proud of her when they found out she was playing in the match. But the shot had smacked Sally so hard in the head, she wasn't able to play on.

2-4.

With roll-on substitutions allowed, Millie was able to come back on and Hannah moved into the goal. The gloves were slightly too big for her hands, but she made do. She had played there before and was happy to help the team out.

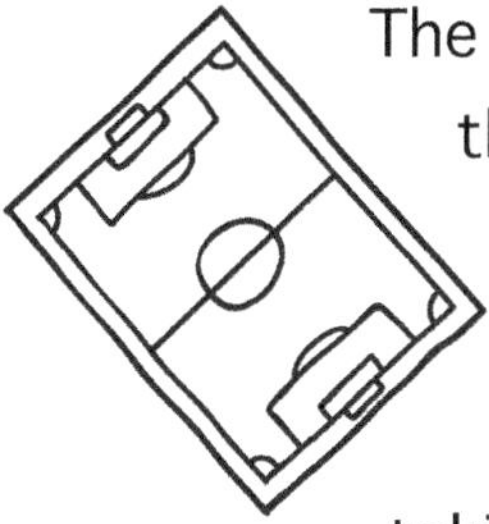

The teams were fairly even for the next five minutes and both teams had come close to scoring again. Millie and Florence were taking it in turns to mark Amy and were trying hard to tackle her before she could unleash another rocket shot. It wasn't easy as Amy was almost a foot taller than them, but they stuck to their task.

Amy was getting frustrated by the extra attention she was receiving and bundled over Millie in a tackle. It looked like she had tried to win the ball too aggressively leaving

Millie in a sorry state on the floor. In the heavy tackle, Millie had twisted her ankle and wasn't able to continue.

Miss Hedges turned to get Tamara to come back onto the pitch but couldn't see her. "Has anyone seen Tamara?" she called out to the other parents.

That's when Martha's dad said, "Yeah I saw her and her Mum heading out, something about needing to get to an appointment or something?"

"Oh, bum!" Miss Hedges realised that she knew about the appointment but had lost track of the time. "Simon, with two girls injured and one girl having to leave for an appointment, can we see out the last 10 minutes with 4 a side? It is just a friendly after all and it would keep it even."

Mr Silverthorn laughed, "This is always the problem when I come here, you are always after special treatment. Why would I want to help you out? I don't think so. Carry on or give up."

Florence couldn't believe she had heard an actual real teacher be so mean to them and their teacher!

Miss Hedges was seething but stayed calm when speaking to the girls. "Ok girls, we only have 4 players now. Would you like to carry on against 5 of the other team or stop the game now?"

The girls looked at each other and put their hands in together, “Come on girls, we can still do this!’ Hannah called out.

The girls were happy to carry on playing. But being a player down was hard, the girls struggled to mark Amy as much giving her lots more space and time on the ball.

The flood gates opened but instead of water flowing in, it was goals galore.

Amy of St. Johns was scoring for fun. She was having a good time, as were her teammates - not that they were doing much at this stage. Amy was destroying the home team all by herself.

Full Time. 2-9.

SEA
BREEZE
JUNIOR SCHOOL

Chapter 8

Assembly

Florence would usually go to school with her mum and brother but her mum was having to start work early today, so Hannah's mum was doing the school run instead. Their families lived just across the road from each other.

In the assembly that morning, Mr Kilman was coming to the end. It was at the point in the assembly where he announces the previous week's sporting results. Hannah and Florence glanced at each other, they were not looking forward to this moment.

"And also the super talented year three girls played their first-ever football match for the school against our favourites, St. Johns."

Some of the year 6 children were heard booing. This was quickly followed by the sound of 'shhhh' from the surrounding teachers.

"Yes, yes, thank you year 6. We came ever so close to beating St. Johns. Sadly though, they lost 9-2 after a hard-fought performance. I was super proud of all of the girls."

The girls sitting in the third row back in the hall were quite confused.

“A good score?” Florence whispered to Millie and she just shrugged her shoulders.

Back in the classroom, Aanya quizzed Miss Hedges. “The closest to beating them for the first time? But we lost 9-2 Miss Hedges. That’s not close.”

Miss Hedges smiled at her, “well it might not be a close scoreline to you but that was the first time we’ve even scored one goal against them! Last year we lost 13-0!”

SEA
BREEZE
JUNIOR SCHOOL

Chapter 9

Junior Governor's Meeting

"I just don't see how they could say no to our request. It isn't like we are being unfair." Florence looked over Millie's shoulder. "Look, there's Bradley. Surely he will support us?"

As Bradley walked past, Aanya blocked his way, "Hey Brad, so we want to play football at break time a bit more, just us girls. Maybe we take it in turns? Every other break time we swap? Florence is going to bring it up at the Junior Governors meeting this afternoon. You'll vote yes right?"

"Erm, what? So the boys would get the football pitch to themselves every other break time?" he said with half a smile on his face.

"Yeah, that's right." Hannah chipped in.

"Well, I think more boys are interested in football than girls, so how about we suggest boy's football Monday, Wednesday and Friday and then girl's football Tuesday and Thursday?"

Florence was studying Bradley's face, it seemed like he had already thought about it. "Yeah, that sounds good," she added.

The Junior Governor's meeting was being held in the upstairs meeting room. Florence had never been up there before, she was excited to see what it looked like.

Often children would walk past the stairs and come up with stories about what was up there. James had told her once that it was where they took all the misbehaving year sixes and tied them to a chair. Martha had other ideas and told her it was where the teachers held secret parties when the children had gone home.

Florence had liked to believe it was the secret parties!

The meeting room was fresh and clean, with a large oval-shaped wooden table placed right in the centre. Mr Kilman was already there and there weren't many seats left - it was very busy. Florence looked around the room and found a seat. The children were quietly chatting waiting for it to start.

Mr Kilman began the meeting, "Thank you for coming, everyone. We have three things to discuss today and I am looking forward to hearing your opinions. First up, new school uniform for September. We have two choices to vote on."

He pointed at two sealed bags in front of him.

Mr Kilman continued, "Secondly, we will be discussing and voting on whether we alter how many times the girls and boys get to use the playground football pitch since we cannot have a second pitch put in. There just isn't space."

Florence was sure he had looked directly at her when he said it but she couldn't be certain.

Mr Kilman finished off, "And lastly, we need to discuss what music you want to hear at this year's School Disco!"

The first part of the meeting was thrilling. All of the children took turns to touch and feel the two new uniform options. One was a dark blue blazer with purple edging and a matching purple tie, whereas the other was a deep purple traditional school jumper, similar to the current uniform. The children voted unanimously for the blazer and tie. Almost all of the children agreed, except for Eddie.

He had an opinion on just about everything and usually, a miserable opinion thought Florence.

Mr Kilman explained the next proposal had been put forward by Florence in year 3 and asked her if she wanted to say a few words about it.

Florence looked surprised, she wasn't expecting to have to speak in front of everyone.

"Errrr, well, I...errr," She glanced around the room to see all eyes on her, "I, errr, I play for the girl's football team, and erm, we don't really get a look in on the football

pitch at break times as the boys are already playing on it."

A larger boy, possibly year 5, interrupted, "Yeah, but girls can play too if they want to. It's not like it is just for boys is it."

"Alright Alfie, that's enough," Mr Kilman called out.

Florence continued, "Yes, you are right. Boys and girls can play football together on the school playground but most girls will tell you they don't want to play with the boys, its too aggressive, too busy and they never

even get a chance to touch the ball as most of the boys don't pass to the girls."
Before the larger boy could speak again, she carried on.

"And I know that more girls would play football if we had it just for the girls. Just one break time a week out of five isn't enough. I think two break times a week is fairer. If the girls don't use it then fine, we will hand it back to the boys. But I know they will. We would have more girls than ever playing - which will help the school team get better too!"

Florence was proud of her new found confidence, the older boy had sparked something in her.

A group of girls from year 6 started clapping, and then it rippled across the whole room. Florence went red in the face and sat down quickly, a voice whispered from behind her, "I think you'll get what you want now!" She turned to see Brad smiling. Florence nodded in reply.

"Ok, well done, that was certainly passionate Florence. I think we all understand the reasons behind your idea. Let us vote. Hands up for yes, we should have two break times for girls only football each week."

Florence wanted to hide. Her friends were relying on her. Her eyes quickly darted left to right from behind her fingers. She was avoiding eye contact with everyone. Then she realised something.

Almost every Junior Governor agreed and voted yes, even the older boy who had disagreed earlier. She could've cried but she didn't. Her face hurt too much to cry anyway because of the enormous smile that had appeared on her face.

That evening Florence was having dinner with her Mum, Dad and little brother Arthur. She hadn't told any of them about what had happened in the meeting. She had a feeling her Dad already knew. Miss Hedges had even got the class to give her a round of applause as a well done for changing the school rules for the better.

"Anything you want to tell your Mum, Florence?" her Dad winked at her as he spoke.

So he does know, thought Florence.

“Oh, what’s this about Florence? Something happen at school today? Football news?” Mum knew that most exciting news from Florence seemed to be linked to football somehow.

Arthur had other ideas, “Did you do a big poo in your classroom?”

Dad tried hard to hide his laughter, “No Arthur, not that kind of thing!”

“Well, I had that Junior Governor meeting today with Mr Kilman and the other Junior Governors,” Florence began, “and he got us to vote on my idea to let the girls use the football pitch for more break times without the boys.”

"Ah yes I remember, I didn't know that was today. So, go on then, what happened?" Asked Mum whilst putting another piece of broccoli in her mouth.

"Everyone voted and then Mr Kilman said enough had voted for it to happen. So it means that now girls get to play football two break times a week without any boys hogging the pitch." Florence was beaming, she couldn't help smiling every time she thought about it.

"That is amazing Florence, a huge well done. And in celebration of this news..." Mum got up out of her seat and headed for the kitchen before quickly returning with a huge bowl of ice cream, "Here is a bowl of ice cream for us all to share!"

SEA
BREEZE
JUNIOR SCHOOL

Chapter 10

Hospital Trip

The girls had been enjoying the extra football break times, and there had been over 20 girls playing every time. Lots of the girls had never played football before. However, during the last break time, Lily had hurt herself quite badly.

She had dived across to make a great one-handed save from an Aanya shot, forgetting she was playing on concrete. Her shoulder, and head, slammed into the hard floor and she had knocked herself out.

She had only been out for a few seconds and opened her eyes to see a blurry, concerned Mr Kilman asking for someone to call an ambulance.

She had been at the hospital for many hours now, but her head was feeling ok and the shoulder wasn't hurting quite so much.

Lily didn't like hospitals at night. She didn't like them any time of the day. The last time she set foot in one was when her Dad had passed away. She always felt strange, the busy, hustle-bustle of the corridors, the different coloured uniforms. The smell of cleaning products was everywhere you went. It was all a bit too much.

A tear came to her eye as she thought about her Dad. At that moment, her Mum returned from the shop by the main entrance of the hospital.

“I’ve picked you up the latest football magazine from the shop downstairs and a small packet of...” her Mum stopped speaking as she noticed the tears in Lily’s eyes.

“Oh, Lily, what’s happened? Here, let me get you a tissue.” Her mum grabbed the tissue box from a side cupboard next to the bed and passed it to her before giving her a big hug.

“Nothing Mum. I just don’t like hospitals, when can we go home?” Lily replied whilst wiping her tears away.

Her Mum sat in the chair alongside the bed, "Soon love, just waiting for the final all-clear from the X-Ray on your shoulder and then we can go home. The doctor said we need to watch you for any signs of concussion, so if you start to feel sick please let me know. It shouldn't be too long now."

Her Mum was right, they got back around 9 PM that night. Lily was promised by her Nan, who was currently staying with them, that she didn't have to go to school the next day.

"Just rest, relax and ice cream!" Her Nan said to her when they walked through the front door. That had made Lily smile and she went to bed a lot happier.

SEA
BREEZE
JUNIOR SCHOOL

Chapter 11

Three Weeks Later

Lily was surprised to see that her nan was picking her up from school. She had only ever done it once before. Lily loved spending time with her Nan. Since her Grandad had passed away a few years ago, she hated thinking of her Nan being lonely, so would make sure if she hadn't seen her she would at least call her.

Everything was always calmer with Nan around. She had loved that her Nan had been staying at her house.

Lily waved and ran over, giving her Nan a huge hug. “Hi Nan, where’s Mum?” She asked.

“She’s at home, love. Not feeling too well so asked me to collect you.” Her Nan replied.

“Oh ok, is she really poorly?” Lily was worried.

Taking hold of Lily’s hand, her Nan settled her worries, “Oh no no, nothing serious. She just needed a rest, she’ll be fine soon enough.”

Her Nan's smile was enough to calm even the biggest concerns.

When they got home, Lily's mum came to the door. She had been crying.

"Had a good day Lily?" Her mum asked.

"Yeah, not bad. My football boots have a massive hole in them though. I need to get some new ones ready for the game on Friday." Lily realised she hadn't asked how her mum was feeling. "You feeling better, mum?"

Her mum burst into tears. "I'm so sorry Lily. I've lost my job. I was so upset about letting you down I didn't want to come to stand in front of all those parents."

"Now, come on girls. We are all in this together. Don't worry, we will sort it out," Nan took control, "I'll put the kettle on."

The next day at school, Lily told her friends that she couldn't play in Friday's game. She explained that her mum had lost her job and they couldn't afford new boots for Friday. Her old boots were no good to play in anymore.

The girls asked Miss Hedges for some ideas to help their friend out.

"What about the lost property box? Maybe she could borrow an unclaimed pair for the game and then return them afterwards?" Miss Hedges suggested.

"Great idea! Thank you, Miss Hedges." Millie said, giving Miss Hedges a high five on the way out.

They dug about in the lost property box which was found outside the front office. They found a pair of boots, slightly small but they were in excellent condition.

Aanya held them up by the laces, "We can take these for Lily to use, I'm sure she will love them."

SEA
BREEZE
JUNIOR SCHOOL

Chapter 12

First Round of the Cup

The first round of the cup. The changing room was hidden behind some trees at the back of the field. It was bitterly cold that afternoon, even inside! The icy wind blew under the loosely fitting door.

The path to the pitch was lightly covered with snow and the frozen leaves on the trees, glistened in the winter sunshine.

Lily in goal was as cold as a statue made of ice - to make her feel even colder she had nothing to do the whole game! Luckily Miss Hedges had noticed, and for the last five minutes, she took Lily out of goal and put her upfront with Florence instead.

With two early goals from Millie, then another double from Aanya, the game was a comfortable win. Miss Hedges told the girls afterwards that most of the Leafton team had never played a football match against a team before and they had loved the experience.

Seabreeze Junior School 4 - 0 Leafton

Millie ‘4, ‘7

Aanya ’12, '15

In assembly, the following week, a positively bouncing Mr Kilman could hardly contain his excitement, “What a win! Next up in the semi-finals, East Woods Primary!”

He asked all of the team to stand up and the whole school gave them a round of applause.

SEA
BREEZE
JUNIOR SCHOOL

Chapter 13

Semi-Finals

St. Johns were playing their semi-final at the same venue (and at the same time) as Seabreeze. The pitches were next to each other.

East Woods Primary was a decent team. Miss Hedges had told the girls that they had reached the cup final last season. They played in a dark green shirt, black shorts and black socks. Hannah had picked up an injury at football club, so was replaced by Martha.

Seabreeze lined up as follows:

Lily

Aanya Ellie

Martha Florence

Subs:
Millie
Tamara

It didn't take long for Aanya to get back into the goalscoring habit as she helped Seabreeze to an early lead. She took a touch around the defender on the edge of the box and then blasted the ball across the goalkeeper - into the far corner.

Seabreeze Junior School 1 - 0 East Woods

Aanya '2

East Woods had won 5-4 in their last game, so the girls knew they could score lots of goals. They needed to be at their best the whole game.

Seabreeze's hopes for reaching the cup final took a backwards step when East Woods scored just before half time. A moment of quality from East Woods' striker, taking the ball comfortably past Ellie and Martha before placing the ball hard and low under the diving Lily who couldn't keep the ball out.

Seabreeze Junior School 1 - 1 East Woods
Aanya '2 Goal '14

Tamara came on for Hannah at the start of the second half. Within minutes of the restart, she got onto the end of a cross from Florence and made it 2-1 to Seabreeze with her first touch. It was a special moment for Tamara as she had never scored for the school team before.

Seabreeze Junior School 2 - 1 East Woods
Aanya '2 Goal '14
Tamara '18

The game finished nervously and Lily was called into action, making two quick-fire saves, following a dangerous corner that had been whipped in from the right. The girls held firm though, confirming their place in the cup final.

St. Johns, on the pitch next door, were winning their game comfortably. The girls from Monarch Academy were struggling to get going at all. St. Johns' star striker, Amy, had scored 7 goals in an 11-0 thrashing.

At the end of their game, Amy didn't join in with the celebrations. She was pleased her team had managed to win and were going to be playing in the final next week but she couldn't disguise her sadness anymore. She felt completely disconnected from the team.

She had tried to talk to her teacher about it. To tell him that she didn't want to cheat and pretend she was a year three anymore.

He had ignored her and told her to stop being so soft.

No one noticed her slip away to the changing rooms amongst the celebrating children and parents. Her sadness turned to anger as she threw her boots and they smashed against the door.

At that moment, Amy broke down into tears.

Multiple thoughts raced through her mind. Should she just do what Mr. Silverthorn had told her to? Who could she speak to? Should she tell her parents?

“WHY AM I BEING ASKED TO CHEAT?” Amy shouted to the empty changing room. She then collapsed into a heap in the corner and started to cry.

Florence and her friends trudged across the grass pitch heading towards the changing room.

CRASH! SMASH! “AHHHHH!” was heard in the distance.

The girls looked at each other, concerned. The noises were coming from inside the changing rooms. The group all scrabbled into the door to see what was going on. Sat in the corner, sobbing away, was Amy, from the St. Johns team.

Amy confessed she was a year 4, not a year 3. She explained that she was being forced to play for both school teams and was finding it too much. She was exhausted and didn't like being a cheat. After talking with the other girls she decided to tell her Headteacher, Mr Smith, about what had been going on.

She knew it was the right thing to do and was thankful that the girls from Seabreeze had been so kind and understanding to her. She was excited as well because she had arranged to meet up with her new friends at the park that afternoon.

SEA
BREEZE
JUNIOR SCHOOL

Chapter 14

Mr Smith's Office

Mr Silverthorn was summoned to Mr Smith's office the following morning. Mr Silverthorn wasn't sure what it was about, he felt maybe it was to do with the recent success of the football team.

"Maybe he wants to congratulate me?" He had thought whilst walking along the corridor. Mr Silverthorn had worked at the school for 3 years now and had a good relationship with the Headteacher.

As soon as he put his hand onto the door handle and looked through the glass pane, he could see straight away that Mr Smith wasn't happy. He pushed open the heavy door and made his way inside.

"Ah, Simon. Thanks for coming. I need you to clear something up for me. I've had an email from Amy's mum about the girl's football," Mr Smith pointed at his laptop screen. "She has said you've been taking her for year three football matches when she thought it was for year four matches. Can you clarify where the error is before I reply to her?"

“Well, Sam, the thing is, the current year 3 girl’s team isn’t good enough and...” Mr Silverthorn tried to justify it but was cut short by Mr Smith.

“Oh, my giddy aunt. You can’t be serious? What were you thinking?” gasped Mr Smith. “We are winners at St. Johns but we only win fairly, we are NOT cheaters.”

The head shook his head in despair, “Oh man! This is going to cause us big problems if we don’t deal with it properly.”

Mr Silverthorn looked down at his shoes and his face had turned a deep scarlet colour.

“We could be kicked out of the cup final!”

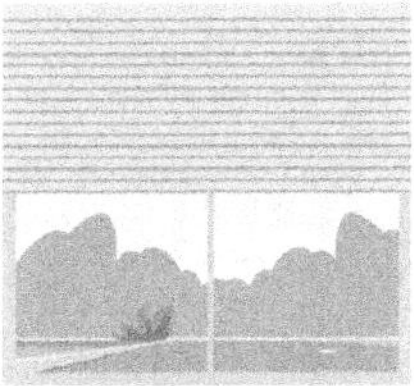

The head stood staring out of his window, which looked onto the playground. "I'll also have to explain this to the Chair of Governors."

Mr Smith took a deep breath, "I'll call Mr Kilman and try to sort it out. But I tell you this now, you will not be at that cup final. I'm not sure you should do any of the school teams anymore."

"Who will take charge of the..." Mr Silverthorn was cut short by Mr Smith before he finished his question.

"Not you, I'll take the team. I'll make sure the school is represented correctly." Mr Silverthorn went to leave when the

Headteacher added, "I'll let you know what the Chair of Governors and I decide."

SEA
BREEZE
JUNIOR SCHOOL

Chapter 15

Pre-Game: Cup Final Day

A week later and the car park at the local football club was full, as were all of the surrounding roads. The girls looked out of the school minibus to see that there were parents and children everywhere.

Miss Hedges had asked Mr Kilman to drive them on the school minibus so they could travel together and it was a good job they had a reserved parking space ready for them. It seemed that the whole town was going to be watching the game!

Building up to this moment, the children at school had not stopped talking about the coming match. Even the boys were excited! No team from their school had ever beaten St. John's Primary School before, could the year 3 girl's team make history?

That was the question that had been on everyone's lips all week.

There were some key changes that Miss Hedges had made since the last time they played St. John's.

Here was the lineup:

Lily

Aanya Tamara

Millie Florence

Subs:
Hannah
Ellie

All of the girls were so excited that Hannah had managed to recover from her injury to play today. She had missed the semi-final and Aanya was looking forward to her first game against St. Johns as she hadn't been chosen for the first game. Florence knew that Aanya could be their secret weapon and could make all the difference.

On the St. John's team were the same faces that had faced them last time, minus Amy. Florence looked across at the team warming up and she counted 5 girls. It seemed they didn't have any subs. She wasn't surprised to see that Mr Silverthorn wasn't there.

"Maybe the extra players are late," she thought.

The team came together for a team talk with Miss Hedges.

"Right girls, you have worked so hard over the past few months and I am so proud you have managed to reach the Year Three Cup Final. By just being here today you have become school legends. The whole school is proud of you and I know Mr Kilman will be willing you on from the sideline."

She signalled over to Mr Kilman who was waving frantically and giving them the big thumbs up. That's when the girl's noticed how many teachers had come to watch. It seemed like half of the school teachers were there and they were holding up a banner which read, 'Seabreeze for the cup!'

Miss Hedges carried on, "I know lots of people have come to watch and that can be a bit scary. But just concentrate on the game, you won't hear them that much. You just go out there, enjoy your football and play like you've shown me in training over the past few months. You play your best when you are all smiling. Trust each other, work hard for each other and remember I don't care what the score is - you are all winners already."

Miss Hedges looked close to tears.

Millie had a few words to say, "Thank you for believing in us and giving us the chance to play for the school team Miss Hedges. We couldn't have got here without you."

Miss Hedges smiled through her watery eyes and thanked them. Out of nowhere, Amy appeared with Mr Kilman next to Miss Hedges.

Amy spoke first, "Just wanted to say good luck girls and thank you for being so kind to me the other day."

The girls smiled back. “Any time,” Florence said.

Mr Kilman then spoke, keeping it short, “Well done for getting to the final girls. We are all so proud of you. Good luck, work hard and enjoy yourself.” All the girls noticed he was holding back the tears.

Mr Smith from St. Johns came over as well, “Just wanted to say well done for reaching the final. I’ve heard some wonderful things about your team and no matter what, I know we are going to have a fun and fair game of football!” He nodded at Mr Kilman as he walked away.

SEA BREEZE

JUNIOR SCHOOL

Chapter 16

Cup Final: The Match

The game kicked off and St. Johns looked hesitant. Millie had taken the kick-off and passed the ball straight to Florence, who took the ball in her stride and drove into their half.

Whilst running through on goal, Florence looked to check her options. The defence had opened up inviting her to continue the charge towards goal. She set herself to strike the ball but her standing foot slipped as she shot the ball.

Florence looked up at the ball in the air, the whole crowd saw it float high and come crashing down past the stranded goalkeeper and into the goal. The crowd went crazy! Florence noticed her brother, Arthur, on the shoulders of her dad chanting, “Go Florence! Go Florence! Go Florence!”

“Great goal, Florence,” Aanya told her whilst fist bumping her team mate.

Seabreeze Junior School 1 - 0 St. Johns
Florence '1

The dark clouds above them had been gathering quickly and it had started to rain. Millie controlled the ball with her right foot and looked across the pitch. She passed to Aanya in the open space but slipped over.

As she fell, she pushed the ball into the path of the St. John's striker who slotted the ball comfortably past Lily from close range. Another huge cheer from the crowd, this time from the St. Johns' supporters.

Seabreeze Junior School 1 - 1 St. Johns
Florence '1 Goal '7

The girls gathered in a circle, "Look girls," Millie said. "It's raining harder now, it's going to be tricky, so we need to concentrate. They are still a good team even though they don't have Amy playing for them anymore."

The whole group nodded in agreement and then they ran back into position.

"Go on girls!" Mr Kilman shouted out from the side of the pitch. The noise of the rain was so loud now that the girls were struggling to hear anything from the crowd. As the game kicked off after the goal, both teams struggled to get the ball under control. The rain was making things tricky. 12 minutes into the first half (which was 15 minutes long) saw Miss Hedges make a double substitution. Hannah and Ellie came on in place of Florence and Millie.

Florence and Millie wished the girls good luck and gave them high fives as they jogged onto the pitch.

"Well done girls, great play so far," Miss Hedges said. "Remember it is rolling subs so we can bring you back on in the second half."

Both girls headed to the side of the pitch underneath an umbrella held up by Millie's Dad.

The first half finished 1-1. Apart from a last-second chance for St. Johns which had been saved well by Lily, not much else happened in the final 3 minutes.

The girls grabbed a drink and a rest, it took them a few moments to notice the rain had stopped and the sun was starting to shine through a break in the clouds.

Miss Hedges took a sip from her take away coffee, "Right girls, same girls who finished the first half are to start the second half. Florence, Millie, you'll come on quite soon."

The girls ran back out onto the now sunny, but still rain-soaked, pitch. St. John's started brightly, Tamara missed a tackle and the forward took the ball past her and passed it into the path of her teammate. Although she was still 12 yards out from the goal, she hammered the ball into the goal.

It flew past Lily and hit the back of the net like a rocket. All the rain water that had rested on the net, sprayed everywhere!

Seabreeze Junior School 1 - 2 St. Johns
Florence '1 Goal '7, '16

Anyone who thought this game was going to be easy without Amy playing, was now realising it wasn't! St. Johns were still a good side; their other players were now getting the chance to shine.

Miss Hedges turned to the girls on the bench, “Right girls, time to get you back on. We’ve got ten minutes left of this game. Enjoy every second of it.”

Florence and Millie jumped up ready to go on in place of Aanya and Ellie. Florence and Hannah were going to be upfront, with Millie and Tamara in defence.

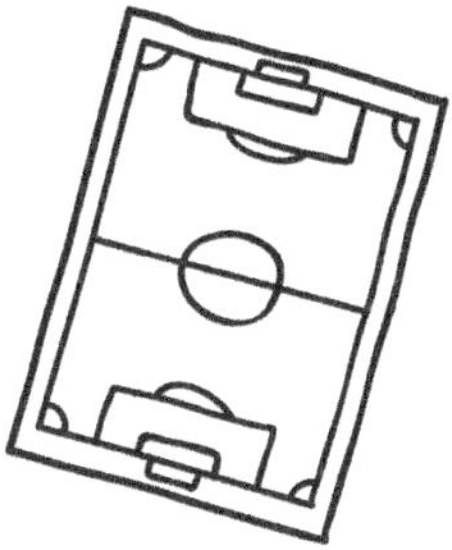

Florence’s team were starting to play the way that had got them to the final. Florence took control of a big dropkick from Lily and ran down the left wing, beating a player and looking up to deliver a cross to the two girls surging into the goalkeeper’s area.

The cross came in and deflected off a defender leading to a corner. A shout came from Mr Kilman, “Remember playtime girls!”

Millie and Florence glanced at each other and knew what to do. As Millie walked past Florence to take the corner she mouthed at Florence, “Controlled and accurate.”

The ball was played across the edge of the box to Florence, who met it first time with the side of her foot. It sailed into the top corner exactly as they had practised.

The parents went crazy with excitement, was there a chance that the girls could win this?

Aanya got the team together, “Lots to do girls, 7 minutes left, let's keep going!”

Seabreeze Junior School 2 - 2 St. Johns
Florence ‘1, ’22 Goal ‘7, ’16

The game had reached a stalemate. Both teams were exhausted and had run out of ideas. A long pump upfield from Millie had skidded across the drying surface towards the keeper, who was unable to control it and sent it out for a corner. Lily looked over to Miss Hedges who was gesturing for the keeper to go forward for the corner.

“Go for it, Lily!” Lily looked round to see her Mum and Nan cheering her on. “Go get us the winner!”

“There are 30 seconds left guys,” Florence called out. “Let's win this!”

The ball was placed down next to the corner flag by Tamara this time. She looked across the pitch to see a packed out box of players, with Florence on the edge of the area. This time she was being marked tightly by a defender - St. Johns had learnt from the previous goal.

Tamara knew she needed to deliver the ball into the area. As the corner came in, the St. Johns goalkeeper rose high to claim the floated cross.

But missed it.

The goal scramble that followed seemed to last forever. The defenders were desperately trying to clear it out, the attackers were desperately trying to poke it in.

The crowd saw the net bulge as the ball struck the back of the goal. No one knew who had got the final touch until Lily came running from the crowd of players jumping into her mum's arms - she had done it. Her Nan wrapped her arms around them both.

Lily had scored the winning goal!

Seabreeze Junior School 3 - 2 St. Johns
Florence ‘1, ’22 Goal ‘7, ’16
Lily ’29

As the full-time whistle blew, Mr Kilman didn’t know what to do, he just ran on to the pitch high fiving everyone and anyone he could see!

After the initial celebration, both teams shook hands and said well done to each other and went to prepare for the award ceremony.

"Girls, that was the most exciting match I think I've ever seen. You were all incredible. You will go down in the school history books. What an achievement." Miss Hedges was getting a bit overwhelmed.

The girls headed towards the organisers, shaking hands with the Town's Mayor before being handed the Champions' Trophy.

Florence couldn't believe what she was holding. She stared at it, the winner's trophy. It was a shimmering, golden, almost magical thing. The feeling had finally sunk in. They had won. The trophy was theirs.

Florence broke down into tears of joy.

Her Dad put his arm round her, "Well done chick, great game, great win!"

"Let's go get pizza!" Arthur shouted from on the top of his Dad's shoulders.

The End

About the Author

Luke Osborne is a Dad and Husband first and a teacher, author and football coach second.

A Junior School teacher himself, with a daughter who loves playing football, he decided to the write the story he could imagine his daughter being a part of. This is his first children's novel, but he has authored other books including:

- Would you rather? Kids Edition
- Would you rather? World's Worst
- The Ultimate guide to Dad's jokes
- 70 ways to promote debate in schools

Thank Yous

Thank you to my wife, Jenny, and children, Florence and Arthur, for their continued support and encouragement.

In particular the children who have listened to me read them the book repeatedly and offered lots of ideas to make it even better. Also Florence, for her love of football which inspired me to write this story.

A huge thanks to my parents for encouraging me to write more and for being a vital set of eyes when proof reading my books. Also a special mention, and thank you, to Heather and Lizzie for the incredible proof reading efforts that made the story even better.

Printed in Great Britain
by Amazon

27329734R00081